SESAME STREET

Featuring Jim Henson's Sesame Street Muppets

Puppy Love

by MADELINE SUNSHINE
Illustrated by CAROL NICKLAUS

This educational book was created in cooperation with the Children's Television Workshop, producers of Sesame Street. Children do not have to watch the television show to benefit from this book. Workshop revenues from this product will be used to help support CTW educational projects.

A SESAME STREET / A GOLDEN BOOK

Published by Western Publishing Company, Inc. in conjunction with Children's Television Workshop. © 1983 Children's Television Workshop. Muppet characters © 1983 Muppets, Inc. All rights reserved. Printed in the U.S.A. No part of this book may be reproduced or copied in any form without written permission from the publisher. Sesame Street® and the Sesame Street sign are trademarks and service marks of Children's Television Workshop. GOLDEN®, GOLDEN & DESIGN®, A LITTLE GOLDEN BOOK®, and A GOLDEN BOOK® are registered trademarks of Western Publishing Company, Inc. Library of Congress Catalog Card Number: 82-83330 ISBN 0-307-01095-3/ ISBN 0-307-60205-2 (lib. bdg.)
R S T

It was a quiet morning on Sesame Street. Ernie and Bert were just finishing breakfast when the telephone rang.

"Hello?" said Ernie. "Um-hm. Sure. Don't worry, you can count on us. Good-by!"

"Ernie, who was that on the phone?" asked Bert. "Who can count on us?"

"That was Barbara," said Ernie. "She called to ask us a favor, and I said we'd do it."

"Oh, good," said Bert. "What kind of favor?"

"Oh, it's nothing much, Bert," said Ernie. "I just said we'd take care of Barbara's dog, Hulk, while she visits her grandmother today."

"Ernie, we don't know the first thing about taking care of dogs!" shouted Bert.

"Don't worry, Bert. There's nothing to it," said Ernie. "Come on. We have to meet Barbara and Hulk."

"Hi, Bert. Hi, Ernie," said Barbara when they all
met in front of Mr. Hooper's store. "I'm glad you
can take care of Hulk. I know you'll do a really
terrific job. I have to go now or I'll miss my bus.
Bye!"

"What are we going to do with this dog, huh,
Ernie?" asked Bert.

"I've got an idea, Bert," said Ernie as he saw
Barkley the dog trotting toward them. "Hi, Barkley.
Bert and I have to take care of this cute little puppy.
Maybe you can give us a hand. I mean paw."

Barkley grabbed Hulk's leash and began leading the puppy down the street.

"Come on, Bert!" shouted Ernie. "Barkley's taking Hulk for a walk. I guess he's trying to tell us that puppies need exercise."

At last Ernie and Bert caught up with the dogs and they all walked to the park.

"Fetch, Hulk! Fetch, Barkley!" shouted Bert, tossing a stick across the lawn.

"Let's play hide and seek!" called Ernie, and he jumped behind a tree. "Bet you can't find me!"

After a while, Ernie and Bert and Barkley
and Hulk plopped down under a shady tree.
"Boy, am I tired and hungry," said Bert.
"Yeah, so am I," said Ernie.

"Come on, Bert," said Ernie. "Let's take Barkley and Hulk home and feed them some lunch. I bet they're hungry, too."

"You were right, Ernie," said Bert, as Barkley and Hulk ate their dog food. "The dogs really were hungry and thirsty!"

"What should we do now, Bert?" asked Ernie,
when they had all finished eating.

Before Bert could figure out an answer, Barkley
dashed out the door and ran down Sesame Street.

"Barkley, wait! Where are you going?" called Bert.

By the time Ernie and Bert and Hulk ran outside, Barkley was back and he was dragging a long, green garden hose.

"Hey, Bert," said Ernie. "Are you thinking what I'm thinking?"

"I don't know, Ernie," said Bert. "What are you thinking?"

"I'm thinking that water washes things," said Ernie.

"You mean things like puppies?" said Bert.

"That's it, Bert," said Ernie. "I'm thinking old Barkley here is telling us that part of taking care of a puppy is keeping him clean. I think he's telling us to give the puppy a bath!"

Bert got the dog shampoo. Ernie got his Rubber
Duckie. They lathered Hulk with soap suds. Then,
while Bert held the puppy gently, Ernie rinsed the suds
off with cool water from the garden hose.

Ernie and Bert dried Hulk and Barkley with
a big towel.

"Now what?" said Bert. "What do we do now?"

"I don't know," said Ernie. "But I think Barkley
does. See? He's brought us his brush."

"He must want us to brush the puppy," said Bert. He picked up the brush and began to smooth out the little dog's fur.

"Oh, wow!" said Ernie. "Look how shiny and soft Hulk's coat is getting."

"Right, Ernie," said Bert. "Let's brush Barkley next."

When Ernie and Bert had brushed both dogs, they decided to go back inside. Bert set Hulk down in the middle of the living room floor. Hulk yawned a big yawn.

"Hey, Ernie," said Bert. "I just thought of something else we could do."

"What's that?" said Ernie.

"We can make the puppy a bed," Bert answered. "We can use this nifty blanket and make him a nice, soft place to sleep."

"Gee, Bert, a nap's not a bad idea," said Ernie
when the dogs were asleep. "In fact, I wouldn't mind
a little nap myself."

But Ernie didn't rest for very long.

"Bert? Ernie?" called Barbara from outside. "I've
come to pick up Hulk."

"We'll be right down," Bert shouted back.

"Hi, Hulk!" said Barbara. "It looks like you've had a good time. Thanks, Ernie. Thanks, Bert. Thanks, Barkley!"

"Aw, it was nothing," said Bert. "We just took him for a walk and played games with him and fed him lunch."

"And washed him and brushed him and let him take a nap," said Ernie.

"And now we're going to miss him," they both said.

"You know, Ernie," said Bert, "taking care of a pet is a lot of work, but it's also a lot of fun. It sure is going to be lonely around here without a dog to take care of."

"Don't worry about it, Bert," said Ernie. "I have a feeling that we're going to have a dog to take care of very soon!"